# IN MEMORY OF JOHN'S MARVELOUS MUSTACHE

Published in Canada by Tundra Books, a division of Random House of Canada Limited,
One Toronto Street, Suite 300, Toronto, Ontario M5C 2V6

Published in the United States by Tundra Books of Northern New York,
P.O. Box 1030, Plattsburgh, New York 12901

Library of Congress Control Number: 2012955642

Library and Archives Canada Cataloguing in Publication

Clanton, Ben, 1988-
        Mo's mustache / written and illustrated by Ben Clanton.

ISBN 978-1-77049-538-8. - ISBN 978-1-77049-540-1 (EPUB)

        I. Title.

PZ7.C523Mo 2013            j813'.6            C2012-908530-8

Edited by Tara Walker
Designed by Ben Clanton and Andrew Roberts
The artwork in this book was rendered in watercolor and ink using a mustache as a brush.
The text is set in Paris Serif and Underwood Champion.

www.tundrabooks.com

Printed and bound in China

1  2  3  4  5  6                18  17  16  15  14  13

# MO'S MUSTACHE

## BEN CLANTON

tundra books

Mo just got a mustache.

A **BIG**, **BLACK**, *beautiful* mustache.

Everybody likes Mo's mustache.

Now Knot has a mustache.

Tutu too!

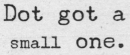

Dot got a
small one.

Nib got
a pink one.

Bob, Bill and Ben all got

EXTRA-LONG and *super-squiggly*

mustaches.

They were on sale!

WHAAA?!

Now **EVERYBODY** has a mustache.

Mo's mustache no longer feels so
**BIG**, **BLACK** or *beautiful*.

So Mo says good-bye to his mustache . . .

. . . and says **hello** to a nice, new scarf.

A LONG, LINED, *lovely* scarf.

Comfy and cozy too!

But soon Dot has a scarf.

REALLY?!

Tutu too!

Knot's is
nicely knotted.

BOOYAH!

Nib has one
with tassels!

Bob, Bill and Ben borrow a scarf
from a snowman. It fits perfectly!

Soon

# EVERYBODY

has a scarf.

Even Imp (the invisible monster)
has a scarf (also invisible).

Mo is not amused.

# EVERYBODY

## explains . . .

Mo had never thought of it that way.

WELL, UH, I . . .

THANKS!

I THINK YOU'RE STYLISH TOO.

HEY, LET'S HAVE A . . .

Suddenly Mo
has an idea.

# FASHION

Tutu's tutu is T-rific.

NIB ROCKS SOCKS.

Dot's hat is all the rage,
and her shoes . . . WOW.

# SHOW!!!

Knot's bowtie is top-KNOTch.

Bob, Bill and Ben go naked.

Imp does too!

BUT THE STAR
OF THE SHOW IS . . .

# MO!

BACK WITH HIS **MUSTACHE!**

*His scarf!*

AND

his BRAND NEW **AFRO** (vintage 1970).

HUZZAH!